Lucky Joe

Leo Jenkins | Brian Kimber | David Rose

Publisher: Dead Reckoning Collective

Book Cover art: Sarah Rosetti
First Edition: December 2020
Printed in the United States of America
ISBN-13: 978-1-7338099-5-5 (*paperback*)

"A clear conscience is the sure sign of a bad memory."
                                                    -Mark Twain

"From this day to the ending of the world…"
                                        -William Shakespeare

"Man is the creature of circumstances."

                                            -Robert Owen

Reader,
In the back of this book is a glossary defining what acronyms await you.

The Bar
USA 2015

Watts being dead was no shocker, Perchigh thinks, but only three? Well, four people if you wanted to count the sleazy rent-a-priest who stayed behind to fumble a eulogy as they left the grave.

Another thing, Joe Watts had opted to be buried in this no-name Middle America town, in one of its unremarkable graveyards.

And, yeah, only three people had shown up. No family members. No childhood friends. Only two alumni of New York's 10th Mountain Division's Alpha Company and one of their Pararescue relievers. It was just Perchigh, Preston, and Ruiz.

The cemetery hadn't just looked old. It looked damn near abandoned.

Except for the clergyman.

He was there, standing, at the appointed day, at the appointed hour, at the head of cheap, above- ground casket with one foot already on the lowering device's hand brake. Yeah, birds sang and all that, but the whole thing had felt somehow *unreal*.

Death had claimed another. Denial always has its various ways, infiltrating the brain. But Perchigh, of all people, he knows what to look for. The smudgy clerical collar—it was like the priest hadn't even been a catholic. And Watts; nobody survives tour after tour just to be ingloriously buried between weathered, civilian headstones.

Once Watts had been lowered, the three mourners had walked to the nearest bar, a midnight-conquers- day watering hole misleadingly called The Prologue. There was nothing that came after a place like this, at least for those calling the stools and high-tops home. Filled with exactly who you'd expect to see in a no- name town, in a leaky loser-bait bar, three Class As walk in, earning the turn of a few necks, and not much else.

Joseph Perchigh is more a stranger to bars than he was to funerals. He'd stood at attention at enough particle-board ceremonies to last two lifetimes. After getting out, he'd mired away in a theological seminary, not excluding himself from churchish mortality duties due of him in an early semester.

Here it comes, Perchigh thinks, some things never—

"God damn, somethings never change," Preston says.

Perchigh never drinks, not even today. His "just water" he'd slipped in the server's ear brought their table two beers and a spartan drink fit for the "born again, bible-beater."

"So," Doc Preston says, "like I was saying, my flight here made an emergency landing." 3rd platoon's former medic, Joey Preston had a penchant for drinking like he needed a medic himself. "No turbulence or anything, but we pulled into Denver like the wings were falling off."

Ruiz takes a sip of his Miller Lite. It was nice to be around these fuckers again, somehow comforting to know that in any other Army doggies' company, Preston's plane debacle would warrant some corny- ass Air Force joke. Ruiz is especially happy to see Preston. A chance encounter OCONUS and the powers of social media had led to a medic's friendship of sorts.

"But it worked out," Preston continues. "They see I'm carrying the uniform, right—on the next outbound. Got here quicker than my original tickets would've." Preston winks at Perchigh, "free drinks, the whole way."

Perchigh is thinking. The spiraling tale of Joe Watts ended a thousand feet from where they sat. In overgrown golf course grass. On a warm sunny morning.

Actually, it ended a week or so ago.

Watts had apparently decided that gun battles and condomless sex with strange women weren't thrill- seeking enough and sought to see if his motorcycle could break Mach 12 while drunk. At least that's what the letter had said.

No phone call.

No worked-up, grieving Facebook thread. Just a brown envelope addressed to him.

Inside it, some typing and a funky watermark on paper that looked like an 8th grader had gone to an office supply store. Perchigh would have never believed it if Preston hadn't called him that very afternoon, in astonishment, asking if he too had received an anonymous letter stating Joe Watts had bit it.

A little searching had dug up that nobody could reach him, even those who still had Watts' number. A little more digging, and Ruiz was on the phone with Preston, confirming he'd also received a letter. Then there were three tickets bought and a closed casket viewing.

But where did the story of Watts begin? That's what Perchigh couldn't help but fixate on. Any tale should, of course, start at its beginning— but that was no easy feat when the person in question was, one, dead, two, something like a pathological liar.

Des Moines.

Missoula.

Albuquerque.

Joe Watts had either lived everywhere, lived more than once, or had the worst memory of any truth- bender in the history of the Army.

He was not just a story-teller, but a godless, wild degenerate.

By what level of our free will shall we be judged? Perchigh loathed his tendency to inner-monologue, over and over. But he couldn't help it, either. *God,* he thinks, *a beer would have me worse right now.* But, yes, free will. That quandary usually, as it did now, mutated quick into an irksome, classic version: *Do we really have free will at all?*

This principle, as old as the universe itself, perhaps older, is why some men were good and others bad. It is why a defendant's intent is a factor in courtrooms and why Perchigh had no problem sending a few people straight to Hell by way of a well- learned M4.

What wasn't so clear is what happens to the moral weight-scale when, say, Watts thermites an old farmer's irrigation system because it amused him... then later saves the life of one of his daydreaming platoon-mates?

As a boy, Perchigh held tight a fear that if you sinned just before dying you were damned. Theology had cleared up that mess, but something of its tangled, twisted logic lingered. Sure, sure, salvation came by grace alone—but some men were more righteous and more wicked than others.

How does one balance a fellow's bravery with his brashness, his fortitude for his seeming joy in causing other's pain, duty for lust, strength for abject weakness... it was these trinkets of the human condition that had troubled Perchigh since boarding his own plane.

Perchigh looks at Preston. Doc's shoulders had thickened since getting out. He'd always maintained the broad, round build of a powerlifter, gut and all. A build he'd since added to, to the chagrin of the seams of his jacket. Then over to Ruiz, a guy who'd been only a vague silhouette on one, far-off evening. Now, hulking and tan, the Airman crinkles his crow's feet when he smiles, joining Preston on their second round.

Perchigh excuses himself.

Why is the toilet the one place you can be honest? Seated, Perchigh takes in the stale-piss and the intellects sharpied all over the walls and the rusted stall door. This dismal ambiance confirms all the more why he avoids places like this, though, with his upbringing, it was hardly a challenge.

Born into a Southern Baptist family and a long line of traditions, his dad had once been an Army chaplain. His grandpa fought in Korea and later used the construction company he'd started to build the very church Perchigh's dad delivers civilian sermons inside each Sunday, back in Huntsville.

But piss and shit and drunks weren't wholly unfamiliar, either. For just as Grandpa Perchigh had proudly snickered—his grandson had decided to join the infantry.

An 11B—the Army grunt—was more accustomed to piss and shit and drunks and lunacy, bloodshed and bruises, late-nights, too many tattoos, women in the barracks, and downright every stripe of debauchery and heathen-sanctioned violence in all that was Christendom.

Or in other words, Joe Watts.

In moments of contemplating a life that's gone, especially a life—though gill-full of lies and nerve- shrieked recklessness—that served with you during your call, a certain shame came with genuine honesty. He never really liked him, Joe. It surprised him then that he'd gotten an invite. A dead brother was still a brother, and paying his last respects was the right thing to do.

So here Perchigh sits, trousers around his ankles, pulled from studying the redaction of the Book of Joshua to pack those previously noted trousers and the rest of a uniform that no longer fit, to board a plane, to be beaten by Mid-American sun, to be pelted by urges to figure out who Watts really was. He opts for wiping his ass and making it back just in time to see Preston and Ruiz's third round go swilling.

"A rare and beautiful madness, that Watts. The world already seems a more sane place in his absence. What a fucking tragedy." Preston laments in his typical poetic way.

"What do you think *he* wants?" says Ruiz.

The sleazy-looking priest had appeared. At the door of The Prologue, the little man still wears his John Bull Top Hat like it is a different damn century. As if reading their minds, the priest takes it off, cupping it under his arm.

The priest sees them. His eyes brighten, and teeth stained by chewing tobacco expose a crooked, cordial smile.

"Hello, boys. Forgot to give you this." In his outstretched hand is an envelope.

It is the exact same brown type envelope the three of them received.

Perchigh, like the rest, was good and out of the military. But some things die hard. He'd been a squad leader. A notable one, too.

Perchigh takes the envelope and flips it right side up. FOR WHOEVER SHOWS THE FUCK UP! Written in that unmistakable chicken-scratch Watts used to leave on MRE boxes and in shitters anywhere from TQ to Bagram.

"Colorful language, I know," says the priest. "But, I know how you boys can be. Served myself, back when. Sorry 'bout your loss."

They wait for the priest to leave, then it is Preston who says it: "Well, you gonna open it, big sarge?"

Joseph Perchigh opens the envelope and pulls out a letter. Ruiz and Preston watch him as he begins to read. "Doc," he says, his face turning white. "You're not going to believe this."

Like a Memory
AFGHANISTAN 2010

Human memory is imperfect. The process requires a person to encode an event throughout different parts of the brain, including the hippocampus, amygdala, cerebellum, and the prefrontal cortex. Before a memory can be recalled, it must first be consolidated. Each time a memory is recalled, it is strengthened and yet altered slightly.

The memory of those mountains, those God-like spires ascending to and piercing the heavens, the rugged taunting allure of their majesty, the fatality of their treacherous sheer cliffs, and Joe Watts, pants around his ankles, bare white ass in the Afghan sun, pissing from one of their peaks while looking back over his shoulder with chipped Cheshire grin, was a memory tattooed on the mind's eye of Joey "Doc" Preston.

For the most part, all of those patrols and missions blurred together. The way university lectures are rarely unique enough through the course of a semester to be individually identified years later. They exist all at once, together yet fragmented. And if combat missions were akin to college lectures, Doc dropped out just shy of his Ph.D.

He'd served three combat deployments with distinction as a Special Operations medic for 3rd Ranger Battalion. At the end of his first enlistment, Preston was offered the opportunity to become the first Ranger to attend the entire 18D course. Graduating that course would all but guarantee an eventual promotion to senior battalion medic.

Fate, however, had a different plan.

Now on his fourth deployment, Doc sat tilted back in his chair, dusty unbloused boots crossed left over right on the shoddy desk, listening to members of 3rd platoon argue on the other side of the ¾ inch plywood wall that divided the sleeping quarters and the aid station.

"I don't give a fuck how many deployments you got. Keep yer god damn hands off my shit."

"Damn. I didn't realize it was that time of the month, Shultz. You want me to go check and see if Doc has a tampon for your bloody pus?"

"Fuck you, Watts. Just stay the fuck away from my footlocker."

It's only been three months; those two are gonna kill each other before we make it to a year, Doc thought as he turned another page in his book.

The remote FOB they called home wasn't much bigger than a high school football stadium. The men living there shared eight shitters, four showers, one DFAC with its seven tables, a cramped gym, and a 300 square foot MWR, complete with 25" television and hundreds of pirated DVDs. The grey HESCO barriers which made up the compound walls completed the prison yard ambiance.

Surprisingly, there'd been no patients for morning sick call. *Must be a light PT day,* Doc thought as he took advantage of the opportunity to read two more chapters. Just as Robert Jordan scrambled uphill, Watts leaned through the aid station doorway, "The fuck you reading, Doc?"

Preston held up the frayed copy of *For Whom the Bell Tolls.*

"Fuck yeah! Love Metallica." Watts grinned, crooked and chipped-toothed. "Hey, chow's almost open. You coming?"

"Yeah, gimme a minute." Since being reassigned to 10th Mountain Division, Preston pretty much kept to himself. Where other members of the prestigious unit felt pride in belonging, Preston felt a degree of shame. He knew he could be a lot worse off after the incident. Hell, he could be in jail. Of course, he made only a slight distinction between that fate and the one he currently occupied. He'd grown accustomed to working with soldiers of a particular dichotomy, being both disciplined and audacious, often at the same time.

Six to eight men sat at each of the seven tables in the cramped chow hall, shoveling their powdered eggs and telling outlandish stories of debauchery and conquest.

Watts was a natural storyteller because he rarely concerned himself with facts. On this particular morning, he was in rare and exquisite form. "No, no, no—listen. When we were in Iraq one night, our Humvee flips into a fucking canal. No, it was mostly reeds, weeds, whatever—anyway — I'm knocked the fuck out. Ammo can got me, or some shit. Fuckin' hero Perchigh comes flying in with his cape, all technicolored like he just came from a pride festival. He pulls me out to the sound of fucking heavenly trumpets and fat little cherubs singing amazing grace or whatever. I come to, and he's crawling on me, trying to give me mouth to mouth. I'm like, 'whoa cowboy. Thanks for the help and all but, I've got an old lady.'" Watts looked across the table at Perchigh. Perchigh kept ignoring him.

After breakfast, the platoon's key leaders gathered in the underground TOC for the daily brief. The bulk of which consisted of Lieutenant Hymen regurgitating OCS jargon while using the word *Hoahh* in place of every punctuation mark in the English language.

The gist of the operation order melted down to, we are going for a walk today. This time to patrol the neighborhood just south of the city. Two squads and a contingent of the Afghan National Police would conduct a six-mile movement on foot. Their presence was a show of force to the Taliban, to let them know that American forces and the ANP controlled the streets. Doc stood in the corner, unseen, unheard and unimpressed during the long and unnecessary op order.

Following the brief, each of the platoon's non- commissioned officers filed out of the TOC and upstairs where the lower enlisted members of 3rd Platoon stood in a gaggle, outside of the ready room, in full kit and Kevlar, awaiting instruction.

"What's the word, Doc?" Shultz called out, seeing the disgruntled look on the medic's face.

"The fuck you think? We're gonna walk around in broad daylight and wait to get shot at...again."

"Let's hope so." Watts chimed in. "My dick only gets hard anymore after seeing a dead body. And I'm getting chafed to fucking death trying to smash this half-filled water balloon all over your pillow, Shultz."

Given his time in service, Watts should have been among the NCO's in the brief. However, he'd lost rank on two different occasions.

One of the incidents happened in the barracks at Fort Drum and had become a thing of legend. The episode involved a tattoo gun, a plus-sized stripper, and a goat someone called Willy. The details of which varied widely, depending on who was telling the story. Watts went on to plead that it was all part of a religious ceremony that was well within his rights to conduct. The chain of command, however, saw things differently. So Watts had the dubious privilege of being the platoon's senior private for the past couple of years running.

Half of the platoon remained at the FOB. They sat around near the motor pool wearing their flak jackets, and were acting as a QRF in the event that 1st and 2nd squad got lit up during their patrol. Two senior members of the ANP walked up front, with 1st squad's squad leader, Staff Sergeant Perchigh, and alpha team leader, Sergeant Stevens, a few paces behind. Shultz and Watts occupied opposite sides of the dirt road several meters behind. They were ten meters in front of the platoon sergeant, RTO, Doc, and the interpreter.

2nd squad, led by Staff Sergeant Bledsoe, brought up the rear of the movement.

Doc scanned every rooftop as the group crisscrossed the narrow, ally like streets. The black, beady eyes of shopkeepers seemed to follow Preston. When he caught one of them staring, Doc silently mouthed, "fuck you." with a smile and a wave. It wasn't that he didn't understand the mission; it's just he hated it. He understood the necessity of working with the locals, but he didn't trust them. He didn't trust them any more than they trusted the Russian looking foreigners, armed to the teeth, carrying fully automatic weapons outside their children's school. So when the LT called an audible and decided to halt the movement so he could sit down and have a cup of tea with one of them, the sound of Doc's teeth grinding could be heard from meters away.

The privates were instructed to pull security. Doc watched several of them pull cameras out and begin taking combat selfies, while others munched on chunks of beef jerky and swilled back Rip-Its.

The pow-wow lasted just long enough to inflate the officer's ego to full capacity. The members of 3rd Platoon once again make their way through the village. An Afghan appears, riding a red motorcycle headlong into the front of the formation, past the ANP, and into the center of 1st squad.

Sergeant Stevens lifts his M4 rifle, pointing it at the man's face. "Stop mother fucker! Stop right fucking there!" The man pulled the brake lever, hard —a cloud of dust spit-up. Half a dozen gun barrels pointed at his head. "Hands up, mother fucker!" The man sat and blinked. "I said, hands fucking up, mother fucker!"

The Platoon Sergeant, Sergeant First Class Mortenson, sends the interrupter up to relay the message. The man's hands raised.

"Get off the bike, mother fucker." The interpreter conveyed most of the message. The man seemed to defy the order with a strange, uncomfortable smile. He began to drop his hands.

Stevens closed the gap. The man put his arms in front of his face. Stevens thrust his barrel at the man's chest, knocking him to the ground. The man curled into the fetal position, hands over his head, the red motorcycle pinning his right leg to the ground.

"What the fuck, Stevens?" The SFC Mortenson cried out.

"He was dropping his hands, Sar'ent."

"Yeah, how else was he supposed to dismount the bike? You fucking idiot."

"I thought, I thought he could be wearing a vest, Sar'ent."

"Doc, check this guy out. Make sure his little bones ain't broken."

"Hooyah, SAR-gent!"

"Knock it off, Preston."

"False motivation is better than no motivation, SAR-gent."

Other than a couple of small scrapes on his elbow and rear fender, the man was okay. It was the closest thing to real combat the new privates had seen. Their adrenaline spiked at the sight of the Afghan being so easily subdued with a single thrust of an M4.

The patrol moved on, hypervigilant now.

A rustle just beyond a berm drew the attention of their gun barrels. A lone goat nearly met his demise as it crested the dirt mound ahead of 1st squad. Three gaunt chickens advanced languidly on the right side of the road. The first two passed by without incident, but the third was not so fortunate and met the toe end of Watts' punt, erupting in a shower of brown and white.

"Watts, knock it the fuck off!" strained the exhausted Platoon Sergeant. As much as Mortenson hated to admit it, the platoon needed Watts. They were down three men with severe dehydration. A result of an intense bout of diarrhea that was going around and that SFC Mortenson was also silently suffering from. The yell drew the attention of most of the men to the center of the formation. Before the chicken feathers could settle onto the dirt road, a loud bang rang out, echoing through the narrow streets.

"Contact—contact! Contact left!" yelled Shultz as he flipped his M4 to semi and began a steady hail of lead projectiles into an already riddled mud-house wall.

The ANP soldiers up front, and several members of the platoon followed suit. Perchigh and Stevens bound forward to the nearest cover while placing rounds on the target building. One of the Afghans up front opened up with the PKM, panic choking the trigger until the barrel turned bright orange. Shultz carried the SAW. He loosed a barrage of belt-fed adrenaline and pent up sexual frustration on the doorway of the shack-like home.

After several hundred rounds impacted the tattered building, Mortenson screamed for a ceasefire. A pair of white man jammies attached to a broom handle was frantically being waved from behind the newly ventilated wall by a grim, ghost- white Afghan man. Apparently, he'd made the untimely mistake of accidentally dropping a large piece of timber on top of some sheet metal that he was using to patch his roof.

"Way to go, hero." Watts said as he slapped Shultz on his back. "You sure showed that piece a shit farmer who the big swinging dick is. You're a shoo-in for team leader now."

"Watts, shut the fuck up." Mortenson commanded without hearing what Watts even said. "Doc, go check and see if there are any casualties. RTO, get on and let the TOC know we are up. No need for additional. We're RTB."

• • •

Weeks later, Shultz was still taking shit from the guys. They hung white flags from his bunk and yelled, "Ceasefire, ceasefire!" every time he'd walk into the MWR or the gym. Watts was by far the worst. He'd start chow hall stories with, "No shit, there I was, man. Surrounded by Haj, steaming hot shit running down my trembling leg, when whooo comes out, guns-a- fucking-blazin'?"

"Shut the fuck up, Watts." Shultz interjected, lifelessly.

"That's right, the Punisher himself, the savior of Alpha Company, the destroyer of walls, striking fear in the hearts of farmers from here to Mazār-i-Sharīf. The one and only…"

Eventually, Shultz was showing up to the aid station almost every morning with a different complaint. Doc had seen his share of malingers. He held a unique hateful empathy for them that only a military medic can have. Preston knew Shultz was just avoiding the platoon. He knew there wasn't anything wrong with him. Preston also remembered the last time he told one of his guys that nothing was wrong with him. He remembered the way his knees buckled, and his body went limp on that mountain. He remembered sticking and resticking the 18 gauge needle into his brother's arm in the back of the dark, thin night air of 14,000 feet, as the CH-47 Chinook helicopter took flight.

"Come on in, Shultz. Sit down. I'll take your vitals. How's your sleep been? How much water are you drinking? What color is your piss?"

Through all the mocking and ridicule, Doc never laughed. Not because he didn't think that some of the jokes were funny, but because he knew the weight of fucking up and letting down your guys in the process. Regardless of why Doc didn't join in on the taunting, Shultz began to really trust Preston.

The Velcro on the blood pressure cuff peeled away from Shultz's arm, "Hey, Doc. Can I ask you something?"

"Yeah, what's that?"

"Why do you hang out with Watts so much? He's a fucking asshole, and you, well, you seem like an alright guy."

"Yeah, well, that right there shows you're a poor judge of character."

"No, seriously."

"I dunno, I guess it goes back to the first day I got to the platoon. I got in just after the company had been released for the weekend. Staff duty showed me to my room. There weren't too many people around. I was exhausted from my drive up from Georgia and Watts offered to help me carry my bags up to the third floor. I said no, but he insisted.

In fact, he just went and grabbed two bags from the back of my truck and brought them up. No sooner did I have the last bag in the room than he handed me a beer. As soon it was half-gone, he handed me another, then another."

Doc couldn't help but laugh. "Now that I think of it, he wasn't wearing a shirt. I kept staring at that terrible Slayer tattoo he has on his chest. He goes, 'Ya like that? Did it myself. Yeah, in my room. I don't remember doing it. I was blacked the fuck out. But when I woke up the gun was still going and there was blood on the floor.' Then he absolutely insisted on showing me Watertown. Wouldn't take no for an answer. He pulled some kind of Jedi mind trick because, before I knew it, we were in a cab headed off base. He tells me his good buddy is the bartender and we'll get hooked up. So we pull up to Joe's Tavern. He struts in like he owns the place, orders shots of Jamo and beers, walks over to the jukebox and puts on an entire Pantera album, then commences to drink more than a sinking whale. An hour later, he's rubbing up on a couple of buffalos. God knows how many drinks after, the four of us were outside, waiting on a cab. The four of us piled in—with Watts up front giving directions and me in the back with the last calls. We drove for a while. I was struggling to keep my eyes open, I remember. I could hear Watts giving the driver the business about something. I had no fucking clue where we were, right. The girls had passed out. My phone starts buzzing. I look at the name and it's fucking him. I didn't even remember giving him my fucking number. 'Shh,' he says all secret like. I see him facing out the passenger side window, whispering into his phone. He goes, 'This guy has been driving in circles. He's trying to fuck us. Take the long way. Rack up the fare. Just follow my lead.' And he hangs up and continues to tell the driver where to go. But he gives him directions to the Subway about a mile from the barracks. As we're pulling in, Watts asks me if I have a twenty. I give him one. He gets out, walks around to the driver side, acts like he's reaching for more money and yells, 'fuck you!' Watts fucking bolts. I hop out and take off, too. The driver tries blocking me and I sidestep him and dash. He chased me. I'm not sure for how long, maybe not even twenty meters, but man, I ran harder than any damn PT test. I had no clue where the fuck I was going. I just tried to keep that crazy blonde fuck in my sights. He darted through some bushes, then I saw him go up and over a ten foot wall like it wasn't even there. Next thing I know we're both standing with our hands on our knees, panting like asthmatics in front of the A-Co barracks. Watts just smiled that smile at me like I'd been the first person to pass selection, and he says to me, 'That's it. That's what being a soldier is about. Not some logo, or the color of your fucking hat. It's about sticking with your boys, getting the upper hand on some asshole trying to fuck you over and fucking them over instead. That's what it is, New Doc. You know that. You be, you have a good night.' He started to walk away, and I was like, 'Hey, ah, you still have my twenty bucks?' He just goes, 'Wha? Fuck you talking bout, New Doc?' and I was like, 'the money. The cab fare.' He patted the outside of his pockets and goes, 'Musta dropped it while I was running. Goodnight, New Doc.' and that was it."

Schultz continued to stare, unable to hide his contempt. "So," he said, "you like the guy 'cause he stole from you?"

"Yeah, maybe. Look, here's some electrolyte tablets. Make sure you are drinking plenty of water. No running today, okay. But you're fine to go do a light workout in the gym."

...

The days of the deployment smeared together. PT in the morning, followed by chow, followed by a mission brief and a patrol, or some form of training. The platoon used a couple of empty houses across the road from the FOB to practice CQB drills. They rehearsed the fundamentals of first aid or took radio classes from the RTO.

The best training days were range days. A line of men stood, expending free government-issued ammo into various targets, propped up against a dirt berm a few klicks from the FOB. Lunch was typically an MRE, and in the afternoons, the platoon would clean their weapons and conduct area beautification, a pleasant way of saying pull weeds and pick up trash.

It was common for at least a dozen or more members of the platoon to pack into the MWR around the old tube TV in the evenings and watch a movie.

The exception was Sunday.

Sunday was a day of rest. Guys wrote letters home, went to the local bazaar to buy trinkets and oddities that they could later claim were the spoils of war. Occasionally there would be a pick up football game. But the best Sundays, the most memorable ones, as was this day, the platoon would have a bar-b-que.

Members of 3rd squad, the pretty squad, laid sunning themselves in the last rays of the late afternoon. 1st and 2nd squad were engaged in the final game of a day-long volleyball tournament. Most of weapons squad sat smoking and joking around the grill. Doc was low in his faded, old camping chair, reading his tattered book.

After dinner, Doc made his way back to those pages, while most of the junior enlisted of his platoon gathered around the low flames of a coveted fire pit.

The boys sat around telling jokes that would make any self-proclaimed 'tolerant' Berkeley student roil with raging antipathy. They laughed and told stories of triumph and folly, but mostly folly. They shared what they'd heard goes on with, and came out from female genitalia in certain parts of Thailand, and many of them vowed right there in the onyx night, under the boundless immortal stars in witness, to visit this perverse holy land at the nearest opportunity.

As the heavy chunks of wood melted into red ember and were replaced by new chunks of wood, the group became smaller and smaller. Until four men sat spitting Copenhagen into the fire.

"Yo, what's up with the Doc?" asked Smith over the violent little pop of receding flames. Smith had been around long enough to feel comfortable asking questions, but not long enough to understand that asking questions isn't necessarily the best way to get accurate answers.

"What'da ya mean?" Replied Jacobs, as he loaded his lower lip with another fat pinch. Jacobs was in weapons squad, and for good reason. He was big and dumb and clumsy and strong.

"I mean, like. He got to the platoon just as we were spinning upright? And he hardly ever talks to anybody. He came over from Ranger batt, right? Like, what the fuck is his deal?"

"I heard he killed a guy," offered Bradley, the prettiest member of 3rd squad.

"Well, that kinda makes sense," chimed in Jacobs. "No, I mean. I heard he fucked up and killed one of his guys or some shit." Bradley continued.

"Oh, fuck, seriously? Now we got him?"

"Nah," said Jones, 2nd squad's 203 gunner. "That's not it. I overheard the CO talking to him right after he got to Drum. I was on CQ. Dude got a DUI."

"That's not so bad."

"They kick you out for that shit there. And it wasn't just that. He blew like a four on the breathalyzer."

"Shit."

"No, that ain't even it." Jones said. "So homeboy gets in a scrap with the MP who pulled him out of his truck, the front end of which was buried into an old ass old oak tree. You ready for this? He was cutting donuts on the front lawn of the God damn post commander General over at Benning. Crashed right there in the fucking front yard."

"Shut the fuck up."

"Yeah, man. He was all passed out as fuck, slumped over the steering wheel when the MPs showed up. Bro, Doc is a strong mother fucker. Put at least one of those fools in the hospital."

"And that's our medic? Like, they sent him to us instead of jail?"

"Yeah man, apparently, he pulled some Command Sergeant Major out of a burning Humvee in Iraq a few years back, or some shit. Saved his ass. Some big hero shit. I don't know. All I know is, dude, is a bit loose."

Smith and the others fell silent, presumably all visualizing the scene of an Army medic beating an MP to a bloody pulp at three o'clock in the morning, while a Two-Star General stood enraged on his front porch in his whitey tighties, demanding reinforcements.

•••

"He's good, Sir. Just a little dehydrated. I'll cinch him up." The platoon moved slowly down the steep embankment and toward the distant village as Doc dropped his aid bag near the RTO and went to work. The altitude was severe in these mountains, 12,000 feet at least, but the midday heat was something entirely ruthless. The RTO smiled at Doc, putting his full faith and trust in steady hands.

A clean, well-dressed man with a gold watch stood out of place amid the dirt floor mud huts of the desolate mountain village.

Coniferous spires scrapped the violet sky.

"He'll be fine."

Helicopters only land in the dark. Safer, somehow. For them. For us. But mostly for them. We wait. Shadow giants drag their clubs from behind titan trees. The sun flees.

He's whispering now, "Doc, help me. Please."

"Gotta get a line in."

"No time! Birds inbound." Calls the LT.

Eyes rolling like bowling balls.

"Load 'em up!" The soft pine needles become

shrapnel in rotor wash. The eye of the storm is
named fuselage or Chinook belly in Native
American. Get there. The sky is angry at us all.
SOMEONE WILL PAY!
The needle slides in and out and in and out of a
tense, young arm. The gurgle is no match for the
roar of a 2,800 hp engine.
Oh fuck. He's violet in the black night. Cast a spell,
make the needle a tube. Ram the throat as the bird
banks hard to the right. Feel the seizing tissue. It's
alright. It's gonna be alright. Solace is no match for
the 2,800 hp engine. I can't find a 10 blade, fuck it.
Where's my knife? Where's the knife? Open your
brother's throat. It's the only way home.
It's blood, not sweat, and you know this even in the
darkness because blood is sticky, and the sweat
ended hours ago. And the mouth is open, and it's
open but not really smiling anymore. So it goes.

• • •

Awoken—Doc made his way from his bunk, under the watchful eye of myriad stars, and into his safe haven.

The FOB gym was an eclectic graveyard of rusted Soviet weights, paired with a couple of cheap Chinese treadmills and elliptical knockoffs. The place was never occupied at 0300, except for

Doc. It was the one hour of his day when he didn't have to play mom—the one hour he didn't have to answer questions like, "Hey Doc, how long does it take for an STD to go away?" Or "Hey, be honest. What's like the worst thing that can happen from swallowing a few of those little packets at the bottom of a bag of chips?"

For years, the act of sinking deeply into his headphones, turning on a playlist of Killswitch Engage, Tool, and 2pac, then loading the bar to its bending point, had been his only catharsis. Well, his only healthy one, at least. At five-nine, a hundred and ninety pounds, he wasn't the biggest guy in the platoon, but he was by far the strongest.

When he awoke in the middle of the night, he'd often walk to the gym feeling like a heavy wool blanket that had been submerged in water. He added plate after 45-pound plate until the bar cried out in the creaking pangs of purposefulness. Every set twisted the soggy blanket, ringing it out a little more, a little more, a little more, until after he'd moved several tons, the sodden, heavy burden of loss, blame, and guilt were puddles on the concrete floor.

Unencumbered by the weight, Doc was free to go about his day in as carefree a manner as any twenty- four-year-old can in a war zone. He opened the 10'x 12' aid station at 0500 and made ready for the first customers of the day.

Doc wasn't surprised to see Shultz this morning. He was actually beginning to like having him around. Sure, he was a little annoying, but it wasn't his fault. Schultz had grown up wanting so badly to be some great soldier. He never could grasp that most great soldiers became so inadvertently. He prepared his entire life for this, his first combat deployment. He'd studied all of the Army regulation manuals and got a fresh high and tight every Sunday through high school. He could recite the Soldier's creed in his sleep and vanquished every obstacle course he put his hands on. He considered himself officer material but celebrated the virtue of first spending time as *one of the guys*.

Doc mixed a protein shake in a water bottle while Shultz began listing off new symptoms. "Look, Shultz," Doc finally said, "I know it can be tough, but you can't let those guys get to you."

"What do you mean?"

"Look, I know how it feels to fuck up, but you can't allow those moments to define you. No one is immune to mistakes. They happen. We're human. The closest inoculate is to learn what you can and leave the rest to the vultures. Eventually, you can become less susceptible to error, but only if you keep exposing yourself."

Shultz's head was down, solemnly looking at the floor, nodding. Shultz deeply admired Preston. He looked up and into the medic's creased eyes and saw his words there, *Don't you even fucking think about hugging me, Private.*

Shultz gave a weak but hopeful smile, "Thanks, Doc," and stepped out of the aid station, leaving Doc to organize various creams and pills as he choked down the chunky contents of a plastic bottle.

• • •

"Alright. Listen up," SFC Mortenson announced to the platoon. "We have intel of a suspected weapons cache in a compound at the center of the village of Haruti. Our objective is to clear and search that compound for weapons. We will be conducting an offset infil and moving in a dismounted patrol to the target building in two separate elements. Element blue will consist of first and second squad, with myself, Doc, and the terp.

"Now that Shultz's tummy is feeling better, first squad is the only one at one hundred percent, so they'll be taking point for element blue.

"Weapons squad and third squad will form element red and move north and parallel blue's position, before sweeping back south toward the target building, providing a moving cordon. Red formation will be led by the LT with the RTO in tow.

"We're rolling out the gate at zero nine-thirty. As always, our role is to provide support for the Afghan National Police. Four ANP officers will be in advance of both blue and red elements. Questions?"

Watts sat up: "Who's on QRF, Sar'ent?"

"The QRF for this mission will consist of two ANP squads, led out by an element from HHC."

"So, the motor pool guys, Sar'ent?"

"Unless there are any other questions, kit the fuck up and be ready to move out in fifteen minutes."

The platoon and their ANP counterparts loaded the four MRAPs and made their way outside the HESCO barriers. They rumbled past barren fields, spitting diesel smoke at dozens of emaciated cows along the way.

After thirty uncomfortable, bone-jarring minutes, the platoon arrived on the outskirts of the village of Haruti. The streets were too narrow for the monstrous, armored, mine-resistant, ambush-protected vehicles.

A small group of Afghan children watched the clunky Americans dismount their iron elephants. One little boy caught Doc's attention. He stood away from the others. He wore a violet hat. His eyes were void of something, curiosity perhaps. The other children clamored about, unsure of themselves in the presence of giants. The boy grinned like déjà vu before turning and walking away.

The platoon split into two groups and began their respective movements to the target house. The pace was slow under the weight of seventy pounds of armor, gear, and ammo per man. The RTOs antenna whipped back and forth, back and forth several feet above the dilapidated walls to the left and right. The corridor was tight. The men were bunched up.

The guys are too close together, Doc thought. *Stay far enough apart, so one shot can't go through two men.* The demoted medic was in no position to be giving tactical advice to the Platoon Sergeant, though. It wasn't necessarily the gap in rank, or the ego of the man in charge, or that Doc was something of a pariah, but more of a combination of the three.

Two kilometers away, element red advanced toward the target building. They passed by a few local shopkeepers, waved, and gave the traditional greeting of *salam*. The soldiers were at ease, joking back and forth as they strolled through the late morning sun.

"Do you hear that?" Doc asked the terp.

The wind rustled the leaves of distant trees. Water trickled through a nearby irrigation ditch.

"No, I hear nothing."

"Exactly. And where are all the children?"

The precarious little street opened up into an unexpected clearing in the middle of the village. The ANP officers lead the way across the one hundred meters of open field. 1st squad fanned out twenty meters behind, with Sergeant Stevens on point. As the ANP reached the other side of the clearing, everyone heard a loud crack.

Schultz looked up, then over his right shoulder at Watts. Schultz froze in place. Eyes wide. Inhaled. Exhaled.

The dirt around Shultz exploded.

A shockwave of disbelief pierced the group. Watts was in motion immediately, leaving safety to cross the forty meters between him and Shultz. Watts knew he got therein five heartbeats. It was five, not four, not six because time slowed to a crawl. As he advanced through raining debris, he counted the red spurts erupting from Shultz's neck.

Watts managed to catch most of the sixth spurt in his palm, but despite his best efforts, he was unable to push the sticky red liquid back into the gaping hole. Watts pressed hard against the exposed carotid artery with one hand and opened his IFAK with the other. The jagged, searing hot metal in Shultz's neck burnt his fingers. Watts pressed harder.

Bullets zipped and impacted the dirt. Watts struggled to open the small package of quick clot, his hands and face already covered in blood.

The rest of the squad was pinned by a hard volley of automatic weapons fire. The trap was sprung.

"Fuck!" Doc yelled. *He's treating in place.*

The command came billowing from the Platoon Sergeant, "Everything you got, third platoon! Give it to those mother fuckers!"

Every rifle, every gun rang out.

Doc knew this was the only moment to go. He'd had just enough time since the impact of the RPG to see that this was a calculated ambush, however. They were trying to draw them out into the open where Shultz lay bleeding to death.

Doc was still deliberating on whether or not to run when he realized his legs had already responded. He slid into Shultz's body like he was stealing second base, grabbed him by the right strap of his flak jacket with his left hand, pulled him up to his feet, and punched his right arm between Shultz's legs. In a breath, Doc had Shultz on his shoulders in a fireman's carry, running back to cover. Watts returned fire, a few steps ahead.

With twenty meters to go, Doc's right foot caught the freshly plowed field. As he fell, a single round panged and ricochet off the side of his Kevlar helmet and lodged into Shultz's leg. Doc hit the mound of earth in front of him with his mouth open. A giant mosquito hovered buzzing in his ear. He tasted potatoes, freshly plucked from his grandfather's farm, and he felt the comfort of a peaceful, warm shower cascading onto his shoulders. It may well have been the only perfect moment in Preston's short life.

From where they stood, the rest of the platoon saw a sniper take Doc out. Another wave of panic hit the men. Watts reached cover just in time to see the reaction on Mortenson's face. Watts turned and took a step into the open. Mortenson grabbed the back of his collar and pulled him back. Watts tried to break his grip, but it was no use.

•••

"He's good, Sir. Just a little dehydrated. I'll cinch him up."

Sixty boots step backward, up a mountain, away from a tiny village, humping packs that get heavier with each meal.

Backdrop peaks made for selfies. No camera for hundreds of perfect miles.

Just one smile—cracked and crooked

Looking over the shoulder. Pissing into oblivion

Invincible derelict, heretic of his own religion

The worst friend—the best brother.

Ropes ropes ropes! Gallows for heroes. Ropes ropes.

The night carries angelic dragons. Their fire breath, belt- fed.

And everyone is alive. Even the ones with severe unknown allergies.

BREAK BREAK

Soap and hot water erase blood but not a medic's
mistake.
Eyes leak, hands shake.
"Doc, go see the Chaplin for Christ's sake."
Gunshot wounds, amputations, blistered feet,
dehydration. Check, roger, check.
Didn't bring medicine, for an allergic reaction.
BREAK BREAK
"Step out of the vehicle. I'm not going to ask you
again."
Groggy. Coming to. "Fuck God and fuck you too."
Hands shake—tight around a violet throat.
Elbow finds its mark in the mist of early Georgia
morning.
He seems so peaceful now, laying there still and
quiet, broken face, broken teeth, flashing red and
blue. Red and blue. Red and blue. Red and blue,
until the colors become one. Until the others come.
Everything lives and dies beneath the rise of a violet
sun.
BREAK BREAK

· · ·

When Doc came to, he heard the clash
of ideology—a cacophony of east versus west.
He reached his right hand forward, clenched at
the sacred earth, and pulled himself a few inches

forward, with Schulz laying across his back. He then extended his left hand and dug his boot in, pulling and pushing his way under the roaring din, the harmony of war. When the men of 3rd Platoon, Alpha Company, 1st Brigade Combat Team saw his labored movement and realized Doc was still alive, they ignited like Thespiae of Thermopylae.

Staff Sergeant Bledsoe commanded his two fire teams to bound forward. Alpha team covered Bravo while they moved. Bravo team dropped and covered Alpha, like the shield and sword of a mighty phalanx, operated by a single mind. The men advanced past Doc and Schultz into the open field, concealed by a terrifying cohesive violence. Watts and Mortenson seized the opportunity to retrieve Doc and Shultz. They dragged the two men back behind cover as 2nd squad continued their advance. Synchronized high explosive 203 rounds sang, *thump-thump – bang- bang,* as the 240 rang. Red team had arrived from the north. Their rounds formed an intersecting field of fire, mixing with Blue.

Doc tossed his aid bag from his shoulders. It was saturated. He peeled the red zippers apart, kneeling beside Shultz's open neck. Doc plunged his hands into the soggy contents of his bag, frantically fishing for a hemostatic dressing and

Kerlix. The wound across the throat of the nineteen-year-old Private First Class from South Bend, Indiana, who had prepared his entire life for this moment, had reopened when Doc fell. Additionally, the bullet meant for Doc's skull found the boy's femoral artery. How lucky. Doc observed his young face, peaceful and white. His mouth opened slightly, like a smile. Like a memory.

The Bar
USA 2015

It was strange, trying to force out some distinct—most distinct—memory of a man so recently passed, and drawing forth rather a menagerie so full of the dead that...

Preston sets down his beer. He looks over at Perchigh but says to Ruiz, "Look at him. What is it, Perch?"

Perchigh now looks over at Ruiz, his face holding the most concentratedly tortured expression Ruiz had ever seen. "I'm sorry, man." Perchigh mutters, "But how well did you know Watts?"

Attention on the Net
AFGHANISTAN 2010 - two months later

Master Sergeant José Ruiz was on his feet. He hadn't been sleeping, not really, more like stuck in that semi-grey area between reality and dreams when the radio next to his head screeched: "Attention on the Net—Attention on the Net—Tokyo, Tokyo, Tokyo."

Shaking off the last vestige of haze, he opened the team room door. As always, the TOC had the hum of ambient light and noise and activity, where nothing ever slept, and there was no tranquility. The call to scramble had gone out, radios were squawking, lots of people were chattering at once. Action was in the air.

Ruiz strode through and opened the TOC door; a gust of wind almost ripped the doorknob from his hand as he stepped out into the darkness, onto the walkway that led to the flight line here at Kandahar airfield. He marched towards the waiting pair of HH-60 Black Hawk helicopters, already with several crewmen scurrying around them like bees. The engines whined. He made out a figure getting into the pilot's seat.

"Spanky," Ruiz said, "what do we got? Anything I have to try hard for?"

Captain Jim "Spanky" Lang laughed as he shrugged himself into his vest. "Nah, man. Word is we have some tenth mountain boys who done fucked up and hit a mine. No troops in contact; maybe you can catch some Zs on the way up there. Going to be about a forty-five-minute flight. Higher is telling us three WIA, stable at scene. Glorified taxi ride, if you ask me."

"Well, shit. Boring's good, right."

Spanky nodded. "I know you guys need your adrenaline fix. Maybe tomorrow." The rotors on the two 60s were already beginning to turn. Ruiz opened the aircraft side door and saw his fellow Pararescuemen and junior partner, Senior Airman Ryan Anderson, already getting into his gear.

"Ryan, you good to go?" shouted Ruiz over the turbines.

Anderson gave him the thumbs up, yelling, "should be quick in and out; I've made comms with the platoon leader; sounds like it's simple medevac!" Anderson was on his first deployment; seemed smart and competent enough. They'd already had a few good missions, dropping into some hot LZs, and the kid had kept his cool.

Ruiz threw on his kit, carefully pre-staged the night before, along with all the rest of their gear. He slung his rifle, turned on his optic, and sat on the floor of the

60. Across the flight line, he could see two more of his fellow PJ settling in. The rotors were turning fast now; the noise and the wind deafened.

Ruiz grabbed the headset dangling from the center console and put it on. "Spanky, we are up in the rear and ready to rock!"

"Roger that, ready to rock." The bird started to push forward.

As with every time he got on a helicopter, Ruiz thought right then, *how the fuck did I end up here, anyway?*

•••

It started innocently enough. Growing up in Tucson, Ruiz was plenty smart, but, as is the way with so many young men, schooling bored him senseless. Sports were his element. He competed in state championships in the 1600-meter race and lettered on the swim team. As high school came to a close, he knew there was zero chance he would be able to sit through four years of college. The military seemed the natural fit. He had heard about the Navy SEAL teams and the Army

Special Forces but had never heard of Air Force Pararescue until a chance encounter with a recruiter at a school event.

Afterward, Ruiz started researching and learned about the long history of the PJs, from their humble origins jumping out of a plane into the jungles of Burma to their heroics in Vietnam. When he read Junger's *The Perfect Storm*, he knew right then and there he wanted to be one doing the next jump.

He enlisted in the Air Force three weeks after graduating. Basic training was pretty much a joke, but Ruiz managed to keep himself in shape by doing extra pushups at night in the barracks. After all, he had to stay in top form before attending the notorious Pararescue Indoctrination Course, the legendary grueling ten-week beat down that all aspiring PJs must complete.

The schoolhouse numbers spoke to the brutality of the training. Here, a graduating class of one. Another with a graduating class of maybe five. There was even the infamous "class that never was" when, out of over a hundred candidates who started, a grand total of zero had finished.

Numbers had improved somewhat with the dawn of the internet age and the rise of the

Special Operations training gurus, but it was still a historical average of an 80% failure rate. It wasn't exactly easy to find legions of young men who could run six miles in under forty-two minutes or to then promptly fin 4000 meters in under eighty.

And all that was just to earn the privilege to graduate. Then the training pipeline started, daunting and endless. Combat Dive school, second only to the Indoctrination course in physical intensity. SERE; freezing in the mountains of Eastern Washington. Airborne, quickly followed by HALO freefall parachuting school. And if you were a physical stud but not so great with the books, you had the dreaded USAF Pararescue medical course awaiting you, a seven-month fire hose of combat medicine, including paramedic rotations in America's big cities to get that blood and piss, real-world experience. If one was steadfast enough to make it through, they then arrived at Kirtland Air Force Base, New Mexico, for the final, so-called "Apprentice course." Weapons, tactics, mountaineering, technical rescue, and eventually running full mission profiles. Finally, just when it seemed it would never end, one day, it did.

Ruiz had been one of the lucky ones, making it through every school on his first attempt. So, the great day came. Students, some of who had been training for over three years, stood in front of their friends and families and donned the coveted maroon beret.

The zenith was short-lived. Joining a team meant being the fucking new guy. Ruiz started from day one, slowly checking boxes as he went out and trained with more experienced men. And the training never ended; there were always more upgrades.

Great wasn't good enough. *Fine, you're jump qualified. Now you have to become a static-line jumpmaster. Oh, you're a static-line jumpmaster? Now it's time to upgrade to freefall jumpmaster. Ah, the freefall jumpmaster is complete; now time for rescue jumpmaster, tandem jumpmaster, bundle jumpmaster.*

Ruiz learned quickly that it was impossible to become skilled at everything; his goal was just to become competent at his tasks and become really, really good at one or two disciplines. He was one of the few who actually enjoyed medicine, so he was sent as the team subject matter expert to all kinds of combat medical training. And then the deployments started. And once they did, they seemingly never stopped.

•••

The two 60s lifted off and away, the roar of the engines cutting through the night as the light from the base faded. Ruiz switched his comm set over to the TOC frequency. "Guardian, Guardian, this is Pedro one five, you copy?"

"Roger Pedro, one-five, we have you loud and clear."

Good, Ruiz thought. Comms had been particularly shitty lately. "Roger. What do we have on our casualties?" Ruiz stared down at the black rushing by.

"Roger Pedro, as of this time, we have three adult male patients, shrapnel. Platoon leader says they hit a mine or IED. How copy, over?

"Roger, Pedro copies three, shrapnel. Keep us posted if anything changes." He reached up to the comm console and switched back to the aircraft freq. "Spanky, you copy all that?"

"Roger, copy all. Twenty minutes out."

Ruiz sighed, watching Anderson fiddle with his gear. It was a perfect shitty medevac call: too long of a ride to keep from getting bored, but too short of a ride to take a nap.

And here he sat, and he thought. There was enough of a moon to make out the mountains silhouetted high above the valley. It was something else, the moon, Afghanistan. *How can it be the same moon that shown down on me at home,* he often thought, *here, in this godforsaken country?*

"We are sixty seconds out," Spanky said.

"Standby."

Ruiz cracked the doors and scanned the sector to the aircraft's three o'clock. Below he could make out the headlights of several MRAPs. Spanky continued, "Sounds like our three patients are stable. You want all PJs on the ground, or you guys want to load and go?"

Ruiz hit the push to talk. "Roger, Spanky. Drop us off, have the other bird racetrack. Let me get a SITREP when I talk to the platoon commander."

"Roger that, we'll drop you and standby."

The Black Hawk hit the ground with a thud, kicking up dust everywhere. Two patients were strapped to litters. Their fellow soldiers huddled over them, shielding them from the sudden storm the birds made. The second aircraft orbited high above as Ruiz and Anderson went boots on the ground.

Ruiz saw one of the soldiers walking towards him. "Good to see you guys!" screamed Sergeant First Class Mortenson over the rotors. "We got a few passengers for you!"

"Roger!" Ruiz shouted back, "same here! Whaddya got for us?"

"Well, nothing too bad this time!" Mortenson said, walking them over to the litters and away from the worst of the noise. "We hit a random goddamn mine if you can believe it. Motherfucker had probably been sitting there for a year. We haven't taken this route before and, of course, the first time—boom. The MRAP took most of it. We had a few guys dismounted, though, and Bradley and Jones here took some hardware in their legs. This is our medic, Preston."

Ruiz nodded, scanning the patients. Bradley and Jones looked up. Both were docile. One grinned and was muttering something. A burly little medic knelt beside them. "Preston, what do we have?"

"Pretty much shrapnel over lower extremities," Doc Preston said without looking up. "We had venous bleeding controlled. No arterial bleeding, but I have double tourniquets on both of them still. They can probably come off if you're good with it."

"Sounds good. Looks like you gave them a dose?" "Yeah, both got lollies." Preston handed Ruiz the empty boxes the fentanyl came in. "I went ahead and taped the pops to their hands. They're feeling good."

Ruiz laughed. "Good job." Anderson appeared, kneeling beside the one they called Bradley. Clapping Preston on the shoulder, Ruiz said, "Okay, let's load these boys up. Ryan—I mean Anderson, get on the horn with Spank. We're loading up with two pax and getting the hell out of here. No need for the other bird."

Anderson nodded, turning away and barking into his radio.

Ruiz turned back to men who had gathered.

"Okay, gents."

A swarm of soldiers started grabbing the Israeli litter handles, grunting as they raised the load. Ruiz looked around, "wait a minute, wasn't there a third?"

Just then, Doc Preston walked over with another soldier. Shrouded in shadow, only blond hair and an arm imprisoned in a bloody sling were evident. "Mister PJ, this is Watts—Watts shut the fuck up! You're going."

"Are you shittin' me?" Watts snarled, trying in vain to lift his wounded arm. "This ain't shit, Doc. I've hurt my arm worse jerkin' off."

It was clear Doc Preston wanted to laugh but didn't. "Yeah," he said, "well jerk off 'til your heart's content in Kandahar." He turned and addressed Ruiz, "you got room for him?"

"...Sure," Ruiz swung his eyes back on the medic, "sure, we can squeeze him in." Extending his hand to Watts, "Hey man, you ready?"

"Whatever," Watts said, walking towards the waiting Black Hawk after using his good hand to shake Ruiz's like a limp fish. The rotors howled. They climbed in. It was tight, but the other patients didn't need much room to lay still and giggle.

Watts sat next to the litter with his back up against the bulkhead. Ruiz tossed him a comms headset. "So a goddamn mine, huh?"

Watts replied, "Hey, aren't you supposed to give me morphine or something. Make this ride worth a shit." Ruiz checked the bandages that Preston had applied to his arm. "I can't believe they're benching me over this."

"Are you in pain?" It was a genuine question. The reality was, no matter how tough this grunt considered himself, his arm had taken a mangling far worse than he let on. "That medic didn't give you anything?"

"Preston," Watts said. "His name is Preston, and he offered."

"And you said no?"

"Well, guess I'll take one now."

Ruiz dug into his kit. He would have insisted this guy get one right from the go, and by doing so now, one fentanyl lollipop made Watts melt, and apparently, Ruiz appear to him far, far more interesting.

What time had passed with the slobbering banter? This guy was a trip, excited as a child when he discovered they had the same tattoo on their inner bicep.

"You're shitting me," Watts said, "exact same fuckin' place, too. I'm gonna get more Metallica- themed work when I get back. You really dig the song, huh?"

Ruiz laughed, now working on a calm and quiet Jones. "Yep, damn small world. But I got to say, the Gadsden flag was around first. Mecrapica came after." Ruiz glanced over at the monitor. Capnography was peaking just beautifully; his patient was breathing fine.

Watts sat back, shaking his head. "That is fucking nuts, man."

Ruiz looked over at Anderson. He was methodically working with his headlamp and tweezers. Ruiz tapped his arm, covering up his headset mic. "Ryan, you good?" Anderson looked over, nodding, screaming, "Yeah, we're good to go! Just picking out some excess metal! No major bleeding! Good vitals!"

"Let's try loosening those tourniquets a half-turn! Watch the vitals for any changes!" Ruiz yelled, then turned back to Watts.

Watts sighed.

Ruiz checked the monitor. BP was holding well, O2 saturation was at 97%. Beautiful. "Watts, something tells me you'll get your chance to get back out there. Hell, I thought the war here would be over like eight years ago."

"Maybe so..." Watts said, his voice trailing off. He glanced out the window before turning back towards Ruiz. "So you just medevac people? Seems like it would get kinda boring."

Ruiz laughed, ruefully. "Yeah, sometimes. It still has its moments, but it's nothing like going out every day and getting into TICs. But that is fine by me; after doing two of those rotations pretty much back to back, I was over it. I plan on having a family. Zero desire to have them being handed a folded-up flag by some General someday."

"Yeah. It'll happen too—fuckin' savages, man. These fuckers can't face us," Watts tapped his bad arm, "so they go with *this* shit. Fuck 'em. We should just glass the place."

Ruiz was intimately familiar with this attitude, especially from ground pounders. It wasn't surprising, especially when people were trying to kill them every day. But there was something about this flight, this cargo.

Maybe it was the result of wondering, wondering which flight would be the one to send him careening into the side of a mountain. Or perhaps too many nostalgic moments, hurling through the air to stop other men from bleeding, had gifted him with something close to wisdom. Preachy—hah!—that's what Anderson had once called it, but it wasn't that. He wasn't trying to impart his elder, ripened thoughts on anyone. He wanted to know what he put his hands to wasn't done in vain. "Yeah," Ruiz said, "well, a lot of them didn't choose this bullshit."

Watts snorted. "Fuck 'em, they made this shithole. These fucks haven't changed in a thousand years. They don't want it to." He looked over at Ruiz, smiling stoned. "Don't tell me you feel sorry for 'em?"

The Black Hawk soared above a small village. Even in the black of night, Ruiz could see the upturned faces as the aircraft sped by. "Well, yeah, a little. A lot of them weren't even born when the Taliban came up. I really doubt they're super stoked on the freaking Taliban coming around and forcing them to do bullshit. I mean, you have to separate the two. The Taliban is the enemy, not the entire country. A lot of them hate those pricks, you know."

"Don't give me that shit. I saw nine-eleven and all them cheering. What the fuck were we supposed to do after that, nothin'?"

"Hell if I know. Maybe we should have just gone scorched earth, you know? Like, come in here, just absolutely crush the Taliban and then leave. Just level the entire place. Kill everyone. Destroy the country. But obviously, we were never going to do that. Instead, it's ten years of this bullshit." He checked his watch. Still some flight time left. "And seeing as how the Towlies control just as much, if not more of the country now than they did pre-invasion... I don't see it ending anytime soon."

Watts laughed, "The mighty US military, still fighting it out with primitives. What the fuck good are stealth bombers if you can't even find a few goat fuckers hiding on a mountain?"

Ruiz checked Jones' bandage. No seeping blood post-tourniquet loosening so far; he relaxed a little. These boys were going to be fine. "You know, they said the same kind of stuff after World War Two, Watts."

"What stuff?"

"Same shit. We had just nuked Japan with this incredible new weapon, the atomic bomb, right? And then, when they didn't surrender fast enough, we decided to nuke them again a few days later. Killed hundreds of thousands of people. Millions, if you count the long-term effects like radiation poisoning and all that bullshit." He peeled some of the bandage that Preston had applied, looking for fresh bleeding; there was nothing but clots and holes. Fantastic.

He continued as he put the bandage back in place. "We thought that was literally the end of war, right?" He looked over at Watts, who was listening intently. "Now, we had this amazing weapon. And the best part is, nobody else had it! We could just bomb the fuck out of whoever pissed us off! Stalin invades another eastern European country? Nuke 'em. A South American county doesn't want to let our fruit companies buy up all their shit for dirt cheap prices? Just drop an A-bomb or two until they remember their priorities."

Ruiz looked down at Bradley. "Bradley!" he yelled, tapping the soldier on the cheek. "You with me? Feeling good? Open your eyes!" Bradley smiled, holding up his hand with the fentanyl lollipop taped to it, making a sort-of *OK* sign before closing his eyes again.

Ruiz returned the *OK*. He turned back to Watts. "Yep, so all our problems were solved. Or so we thought. Because we figured out pretty freaking quick that you can't just drop a nuke on a country if they have an election that doesn't go your way or to squash some small rebellion. You know what I mean? So we weren't going to glass some third world country if they weren't going to play ball with us. So then what? Now we have the most powerful weapons in the world, and we can't do shit with them."

Watts frowned. "I sort of get what you're saying. But we have shit that is way more precise than that now. We have these weapons that can detect when a goddamn mouse farts up in the mountains, and here we are ten years in and can't get rid of some fuckin' boy fuckers hiding out in caves. It's a freakin' joke, man. And fuck the people. They work with these assholes. Hide their weapons. Play stupid when we roll through— shit half of them are Taliban themselves, probably."

Ruiz glanced up at the IV drip chamber. Still dripping away, the vein was still open; good. "Well, honestly, can you blame them? Look at all the shit we've put them through. How would you feel if one day a shitload of foreigners who didn't speak your language just decided to take over your country? And then, further, they often fucked things up completely, bombing the wrong house and shit, killing all kinds of civilians? You'd be pissed off too."

He turned away. He knew, though Anderson couldn't hear it, he was getting a kick out of the talk. But in line with being the new guy himself, Anderson attended to his duties and let his senior man do what he'd been correctly guessing: schooling the damn grunt. Now Anderson wasn't just making good pressure dressing but a work of art. "Honestly, Watts," Ruiz said, "this whole thing... maybe it's just none of our business, and we should've just stayed the hell out."

"Stay out or go all in."

"Yeah, but what does all in eventually mean? It's not like we can round up every man, woman, and child. Would you shoot a kid?"

Watts stared at him a lot longer than the question required.

The flight engineer waved. Ruiz clicked over to the pilot/crew frequency. "José, we're about then minutes out, roger?"

"Roger, copy, ten minutes out. Patients are doing good." Ruiz clicked back over to the comms he and Watts were using. "Don't get me wrong, it's true they are completely fucked up over here. But what are you going to do? Ten years in, not a thing has changed. If anything, it's gotten worse."

Watts nodded, more animated. "Exactly! May as well have some fun."

"Ah, there we go," said Ruiz. A quick glance at the monitor; pressures were still good, respirations had slowed. Bradley was snoring now; a patent airway was all any good medic wanted. "You like war. I get it, but there's nothing that will ever come close to this. You understand you need to feel something else, right? This isn't going to last forever. Or, fuck, who knows. Maybe it will. But either way, you need to have something else to get back to. You married? Kids? Girl?"

Watts shook his head. "Nah, not married. No kids— fuck that."

Ruiz glanced over at Anderson, who flashed five fingers to him, yelling, "Five minutes!" He turned back to Watts. "I'm just saying, give it some thought."

The Black Hawks entered the valley, not long before Kandahar airfield.

Only about sixty seconds to go, Ruiz turned, tapping on Bradley. "You with me?" Bradley opened his eyes sleepily, smiled, giving the thumbs up. A quick check of the monitor: heart rate good, pressure good, O2 stats good, even the capnography was good. All shit that your neighborhood combat medic loved to see. He turned to Watts. "Okay, man, we're about to hit the airfield. You got all your shit? They have a team waiting for us on the runway; they'll take you and your boys from there."

"Can I get another fentanyl? Yeah, yeah, I'm ready to go— kinda stoked to be at a big base for a little while. At least I'll get some decent fucking food."

"Oh yeah, decent chow, for sure." Ruiz paused, pulling out his notebook from his chest rig. The aircraft slowly touched down, and Ruiz gave a silent thank you to the big man in the sky who had let them come home safely one more time. "Listen... I'm going to give you my email."

"I don't have an email," Watts said, getting onto his feet.

"Okay... phone number?"

"Better just make it an address, dude. And what for?"

"Why not? You ever wanna talk some more foreign policy—this time preferably over beers." Ruiz wrote his address down as the aircraft slowly taxied into position. Anderson had already cracked the doors; the hospital staff was out there waiting. The Black Hawk slowed, slowed, and finally came to its halt.

The turbines were winding down as Spanky came over the radio. "Pedro one five, touchdown, mission complete." The waiting hospital crew descended on the Black Hawks, grabbing the patients.

"Anderson, make sure you get a good handoff!" called out Ruiz. The younger PJ nodded, turning towards the doctors and nurses, busily loading the stretchers onto their wheeled cots.

Watts accepted the page that Ruiz had torn from his notebook. "Seriously, man," Ruiz said. "Hit me up. I don't know anyone who doesn't come unglued on a lollipop. You may be a one-man national asset."

"Shit, maybe I'll become a PJ then. Y'all got plenty."

"At medic school, though, they fill your head with empathy crap." He winked at Watts. "You sure you can handle that?"

Watts looked down at the paper. "Master Sergeant Joe-zee Ruiz, I do declare, if I died a sweetheart like you'd actually come to the funeral." And then he strode off to join the hospital team.

"Yeah," he called out, "but let's see that that doesn't happen!"

There goes another, Ruiz thought, grabbing his gear, *another unrepentant asshole that makes the US fighting force unmatched in all history.*

The Bar
USA 2015

Ruiz looks at Perchigh now. Perchigh is still holding the envelope in one hand, the letter in the other. He is reading it again. Ruiz nudges him, "What's up, man? You either seen a ghost or just got orders back to the damn sandbox."

Big Mouth
IRAQ 2005

"Call it in," Perchigh slipped out the front passenger seat, leaving the door open. That his RTO had been asleep, he'd been unaware, the same radio man who now squinted through NVGs at the spinning tires of an upside-down Humvee.

Joseph Perchigh was two things right then: the youngest team leader in 3rd Platoon, and in a full sprint toward a vehicle that had tread too close then flipped into a canal.

Soldiers were already scrambling out; through a door they'd been able to make out in blackness as the least underwater, or they crawled through fetid weeds and out the turret. Some retained their rifles. Some didn't. One hugged a tire, revealing himself by way of a thick Boston accent as Bledsoe, cursing and coughing and laying into his driver.

Depending on a few factors, Iraq could get cold at night. And it was night, and it was most certainly Iraq—in the middle of a cache-riddled farmland surrounding Baghdad. The idiots made their way up the berm, joining their leader, Bledsoe, revealing a team that was one man short.

Perchigh was down the berm and in the water. "Bledsoe!" One flash of white light was all it took. A man was still inside, in the back, half underwater and crushed by loosened cans of 7.62.

"What—who?" Bledsoe was at his elbow. Perchigh slammed his rifle into Bledsoe's chest, crawling inside, tossing away the heavy cans and pulling out a limp Joe Watts.

"Get 'em up—Get Doc—Get down here!"

Commands flew from Perchigh and Bledsoe as the two team leaders dragged Watts up and onto the canal's frontage road.

It should have been Bledsoe doing it, or maybe that careless ass driver, but Perchigh knew Bledsoe was shaken up and that driver's made mistakes and he was already rifle-free, on his knees.

When Watts came to, he did so screaming to life in lung-flung water. Only after Watts' team saw they were up, that they hadn't lost someone to this miserable inglorious death of a drowning, only then did Perchigh feel the pain in his ankle.

"You didn't have your Kevlar on," Bledsoe said, handing Perchigh back his M4 and fuming at Watts. "Did you?"

"Yeah," Watts said, grunting, coming to his feet. "Well," Watts went for a cigarette, but the pack was too wet and Bledsoe knocked it out of his hand, "I tried to bust out a regulation haircut right quick, but ol' dipshit flipped us and wanted to say otherwise."

In every infantry unit, you will have him. In every fighting hole or half-sunken Humvee, chances are that nearby there will be a Watts. Chances are equal that there will also be that guy who doesn't drink, has no tattoos, and most remarkably of all; doesn't partake in the solaces of wartime tobacco. Joseph Perchigh had only been with one woman, actually attended church service back at Drum, and if he cussed at you the degenerates around him knew that the shit had truly hit the fan.

He didn't cuss, at Watts nor at anyone else, but he came damn close.

Perchigh wasn't without his funny bone. Contrary to the group's opinion, he loved dark humor. What he didn't like was shucking off unprofessional behavior, especially when it could cost lives. They were all paid the same. Guys like Bledsoe, they were okay; mistakes happen and nobody can watch everyone all the time. But Watts, he was a cancer.

Soggy and silent, Perchigh left Watts and the rest of Bledsoe's team, making it a single step before realizing that he now had to hide a limp.

Great, Perchigh thought. Only three months in, and now *this*. The gear was heavy enough, especially for a tall, lanky frame. He concentrated, favoring the good one, the one that hadn't gotten twisted while saving someone who probably should have drowned.

The night's mission was a bust. By daybreak, the wrecker had arrived, and by noon a weary platoon abandoned all ideas of glory and hobbled back behind the HESCO barriers.

Back on base, Perchigh was headed straight to the medic station when he was told he was needed in the platoon sergeant's office. He winced when he turned around, wincing further when he heard SFC Gilliard had started without him.

"He joins us. Sit down, Perch." SFC Gilliard hadn't just seen both invasions but had been a drill sergeant down at Benning. He held a coolness that some locked onto, while others, Perchigh among them, viewed him as a ticking time bomb. "We're going back out tonight."

Perchigh listened as Gilliard rehashed the bullet points: Some Marine unit, Radmin or something, had triangulated the position of what was sounding like a low-level commo officer for the Mujahideen. *Big Mouth* was the epitaph they'd given him—carved in stone and now penned on the dry-erase board—and Operation Big Mouth meant driving out to a small village, surrounding it, infiltrating the three houses and hopefully rolling up a shit bag.

"Same route?" someone asked.

"Same route," Gilliard said. Big Mouth reportedly dispensed cell phones in the AO. He, a man in his thirties according to the latest string of sourceless intel, also served as a sort of old-school telephone operator; connecting Muj fuckers from Tikrit to Karbala. Higher didn't just want the man; they wanted the gear. "Meaning we need the phones. So don't go blasting everything to hell." Gilliard repeated, knowing already it was a moot point. "If they'd wanted *that*, they'd have tasked their Marines on it."

Cut loose, the squad and team leaders joined the rest of the platoon in the crap gym, or in the chow hall, or did as Perchigh: shower off and rack the heck out. Amazing what a trailer park could look like in Iraq. Combat Housing Units was what he remembered to call them if talking to the brass, but the white and beaten metal housed three pods, sticks of furniture, and close to double-digits in soldiers. You could identify a neighbor by laugh or protein-powdered fart. A "CHU" was not bad, way better than a tent. Heck, it had air conditioning, most days. Yet, the trailers and their squeezed placement against one another gave a hilarious trashy effect, one not lost on even the dullest gunner.

He shared such a trailer with Bledsoe, who promptly woke him to usher in the daylight before remembering to quietly shut the door. Normally, Bledsoe may have razzed him with "what, no gym?" The meathead tiptoed around their cramped space, shaking a protein-loaded Nalgene with the due given someone whom you are embarrassed to be around.

Perchigh was tempted to tell him he had no reason to be—well, an unsecured ammo can is no bueno, and what the heck—but Watts was an idiot, and it hadn't been him who'd been topsy-turvied. Maybe he also would have been a little slow to act. But the pious and tired of the two retained his thoughts, made all the easier by the renewed throbbing in his ankle. He didn't want to look at it.

No gym, he mused, *funny*. That may be off the schedule for a bit.

Before Bledsoe, for some reason, he had been dreaming of the Adirondacks. It was something like a unit secret; most men at 10th Mountain never got to go to mountain anything. While guys tore off post to try and go "fuck the water buffalos" at Joe's Tavern, Perchigh had spent a considerable amount of time and money putting himself through civilian mountaineering courses. It's funny how memories of fitness can slam home how severe and lingering a new injury may actually be.

Leaving Bledsoe to his Maxim collection, Perchigh soon donned his shades and slowly made his way over to the medics. There he was pestered for exactly forty-seven minutes, his watch confirmed. Watts needed to get his "head examined," a term in usual circumstances that would have sent Perchigh into the rafters. Perchigh's story that he came to check on him was met with instant approval, sending the liar down to levels of a very real but very livable guilt. Finally alone, watching the menace trot off with a bandaged head right out of a cartoon, Perchigh laid on the exam table and did as he was apparently destined: to contemplate life and how darn confusing it could be.

•••

Iraq had been... strange. Thus far, it was like being a cop in a crappy gangland. For all the whispers surrounding Perchigh—Oh, how could he be an alpha male if he didn't drink or bar fight— closet careerist— Christian stuff meant he wouldn't pull the trigger when his time came—for all the gunk uttered below him, and who knew, maybe a few above him did too, the irony was he was drawn to war like a moth to a flame.

Back on Drum, atheist YouTubers used to salivate whenever he'd jump into the feeding frenzy. How they'd gloated, railed in the comments. The Old Testament was rife with warmongering, blood, and murder. And how right they were, though they all always missed the point.

Man was fallen. *Is* fallen. Simple. The path to our righteousness invariably lay strung out over a landscape of hardship, blocked and besieged by those who'd forsaken their own humanity. Those who used a false religion to promote the secular lusts of power and tyranny, they were blockades to none other than God's people, slowly, painfully slowly, shedding blood to see true what Martin Luther King had called the moral arc of the universe.

And this is why Iraq had proved so frustrating.

When they'd gotten close to the airfield, coming into country, it was around 0300. He saw, far down below, the glow of Iraqi settlements. *How many down there want to kill me*, he found himself thinking. *Would we meet? Who'd win?* Screaming, whiplash angles, known euphemistically as "combat maneuvers," and an admin clerk who puked in his SFC Gilliard's helmet later, they were boots on the ground. In Iraq. In the ancient Mesopotamian land that had called him to partake in war.

The sense of destiny was undeniable. A few September 11th's pass, dropout of Bible College, and there he was, riding a great wave.

Like a drug deal in the night, the entire unit grumbled and growled until the convoy stopped at the ominous front of their new home. Gates opened, and before long, they were standing at the shores of a vast trailer park. The outgoing unit had compacted into about half their original berthing, allotting them the other. Crammed into a ten by ten room with his team, sleeping arrangements were dictated by where they could push the guns and maps and water bottles far enough out of their way.

Once settled, something had pulled Perchigh to his feet. He wanted to stretch his legs, but he also wanted to be alone. He needed a moment to absorb that he was, no shit, in a real life combat zone.

Outside, the early night began showing its unpolluted brilliance. The air had that warm, comfortable feel one gets in the few hospitable hours of a desert's transition. Perchigh climbed on top of some HESCO barriers. Lighting a cigarette, Joe Watts climbed the HESCO barriers that Perchigh had thought he'd hidden himself on.

"Hey, Watts," Perchigh sighed.

"Sup dude."

Perchigh had learned quickly to avoid certain people. Back at Drum he'd watched Watts sneak into the barracks a strung out, heroin girl. Then there was that time he and two others showed up to the rifle range a little drunk. But it seemed the rebellious libertine had an undying love for Perchigh. They'd started out as privates together. Out of everyone, they'd known each other the longest, even while one excelled in the regimented life and the other was steadily heading to due punishment.

Together they sat, atop the dust, amidst the hurled piss bottles and the Iraqi sand. Watts took a drag. To the north, .50 cal machine guns were putting out streams of red.

"First two-fifty, most likely," Watts said, taking another drag. Perchigh nodded, remembering proudly a common wartime procedure for the belt-fed. Either a firefight had just erupted, and an initial 250 round-belt of tracers was delivering an elite style of destruction, or a lull in the fight had allowed some guys to restock their big guns. If it was a second tracer belt, it would most likely mean a supporting unit had just arrived.

Perchigh listened. It was too far away— no *thwacks* against walls that stood no chance. As the specks traversed the sky, hugging spaces above the earth, power-line level, Perchigh put together a puzzle of questions and similar answers. He wanted to help whoever was out there. Yeah sure, to assist, but, as clear then as ever, he wanted to get scraped up and earn his stripes.

Those men behind those guns, who were they? Who were they fighting? What were the specifics? A hostile house? Dug in position? Anybody dead?

Watts put out his cigarette. "We're sittin' here, safe an' sound, still smelling like Fort fuckin Drum, and those guys are out there gettin' it."

No sooner had Watts shut up, then a rolling thud of impacts began going off behind them. As sudden to stop as they'd come, all that was left of the mortar attack was gunfire erupting from what sounded like the main gate.

"Sounds like ours." Perchigh said.

"Not too bad for our first night."

A violent roar and a few sputters, then over—what could have been a gate guard valiantly killing a sprinting suicide bomber could have just as likely been a terrified American shooting wildly near a mortar's point of impact. The men of Alpha Company, 3rd Platoon would all soon learn those same mortars ended up taking out a number of people, including a big wig sir and the oncoming sergeant major from some other unit.

"Well, we're here." Perchigh said, struck by a pang of guilt for the excitement in his own voice.

Watts followed him down. Watts cussed, and he howled about how much he agreed with "Perch" and how soon they'd be painting the walls bloody fucking red, then he broke off at the trailers to go do God knows what.

Perchigh was greeted by his team's faces when he swung the door open. Lifted up from maps and portable DVD players, he couldn't help but notice they were all absent the excitement he'd momentarily shared with Watts outside.

Soon came the transition with the outgoing unit. A few images of armored youth, silhouetted against the reds of the Iraqi sunset, and then they were gone. It was 1st Brigade Combat Team's turn, in a hellacious chunk north of the Euphrates.

A month of operations later, the term *transition* had taken on a whole new meaning. Perchigh's platoon had dodged poorly aimed mortars and off-roaded over berms and farmland alike. They had sand in their boots. They'd crawled in the nooks, zip-tying prisoners and parading them in front of wailing women, or they got their Humvees stuck in quicksand and stared awkwardly for hours in a committed silence at their Iraqi attachments.

Cutting their teeth wasn't without its moments of tension, or without its own bizarre hilarity. Most of the senior enlisted had purple hearts. For Perchigh and for the majority of the Company, this was their first time overseas. Eyes glued to the farm huts passing a Humvee window, every type of eye and ear and gear protection tight against their body, seeing a parked tractor, remembering the class on exploding vehicles, and thus the heart rate spikes and *Oh, shit, we are getting close to that thing! Back up!*—small blips of greenhorn paranoia were prevalent, but soon these moments faded. And as they grew accustomed to life in Iraq, the "war" effort revealed itself to be a crudely- defined occupation force.

To those who were there, the sensation of being an underpaid cop in the biggest trash heap on earth sunk in, and hard, down passed the body armor, down passed the swelling spare-tire from excessive MRE exposure, finally resting in the bones.

They weren't some rolling horde of fixed-bayonets, pushing the front-line with every advancing rotation of the Humvee's wheel. That had already been done, a few times, and in a similar fashion to every invading army since the dawn of conquest. But unlike the juicy contents of the history books, they hadn't salted the fertile earth; they hadn't beheaded a surrendered enemy in a theatrical display. No, they found themselves participating in what sometimes felt like schizophrenia.

In one day, a team who'd trained for close to a year to kill the correct people would find themselves passing out packs of cigarettes with hotline numbers to report terrorists, then patrol some farmlands, then get to know the locals, and then hit a seemingly random house full of military-aged males, hoping they would fire back or just have a little useful information. While it may have made sense in theory, in practice the whole thing felt jagged, like someone somewhere was struggling to find their collective purpose, and hadn't yet admitted to themselves that maybe they didn't have one.

The "hearts and minds" slogan was practically etched onto the face of the moon by 3rd Platoon's second month in country.

"We're really making a difference out here," Perchigh had made the mistake of saying to the platoon, trying perhaps to vainly convince himself and instead receiving instant pummeling.

"No we're not," snorted one of his Joes who normally stayed quiet. "They don't give a fuck. None of them understand a word we say either."

"Yeah, maybe," Perchigh deflated. "But we're rolling up bad guys, and they see we aren't bulldozing their mosques."

"I sure thought we were gonna get shot at more," chimed in Watts, who then rolled up his sleeve to expose his favorite tattoo and, of course, to ignite the chorus.

"Screw it!" half the platoon yelled.

Watts smiled back, slapping his forearm and the blasphemy it depicted: a cartoonish screw buried deep in an inverted cross, all below the big, blue, gaudy letters *SKREWWIT*.

Perchigh slinked off.

There was palpable frustration. It seemed to infect some while sparing others. Despite his duty to remain outwardly motivated, Perchigh secretly grew to envy the invasion-era combatants and the retakers of Fallujah; their clear sense of purpose, the chaotic horizon—and then after their third-shift, mall cop brothers were left with knee-jerk nation building. Iraq was given humanitarian injections, and it overdosed the actual ground-pounders.

And then there was the emergence of an enemy weapon, one which not only tore through and maimed thousands, but whose acronym would explode into synonymity with the Global War on Terror itself.

Somewhere in their second month, 3rd Platoon was rolling on top of one of the two berms that held in a canal. Perchigh's vehicle was upfront, taking directions from his squad leader. They were a couple miles south of Baghdad, heading to some forgettable task. The sun had just set. Those who drove wore their NVGs. The rest took in hues of house and car with the naked eye. The platoon had been outside the wire for a few days by then, and to Perchigh's best recollection, they'd spent it watching mortars impact, most far away, a few not.

The day prior to them rolling out, Watts and Perchigh had locked horns so bad that the chaplain himself had to intervene. Later that evening, guys from different platoons came up in the chow hall to joke how everyone had seen it, how righteous the fist- fight would have been. It had been a rare moment that made Perchigh not want to be in Iraq, or in his platoon, or even in the Army. He'd been dwelling on it since the shoving match, bouncing back and forward from ashamed he let a string of well-aimed jokes piss him off so bad to wishing he had taken that shot he saw and knocked Watts' ass out cold.

As is the case in such communities, hen-house bullshit took a backseat when there was a job to do. After their spat, they'd worked together as well as they always had, and always would.

Perchigh donned his NVGs. He was right; he had seen a truck. He'd caught out of the corner of his right eye a bongo paralleling them on the opposing berm. Nothing new, it wasn't coming toward them, and they'd occupied a bustling area where vehicles came and went all hours of the day and night. Maybe the first month he would have kicked up a fuss, but time in country gives those that jaded comfort, and fast.

In all actuality, he didn't know what had occurred first. Two memories were conjoined in a sequence possibly rearranged. As he remembered, the bongo truck veered hard right, right off the berm, crashing somewhere below. Then *it* happened.

An IED exploded, directly under Perchigh's Humvee. His consciousness, the thing he defined as "Perchigh," the collection of memories and present thought, went right out behind his wind. It, *Perchigh*, flew out his mouth, up at the ceiling and then came floating down and Perchigh went back in. He was back, helping hold the steering wheel of a moving

Humvee with his left hand. The concussion had turned off his NVGs.

"Everyone all right?!" Perchigh shouted, turning his vision back on then flipping them off his face just as fast.

"I'm... good." "Good."

"Me too."

"What the fuck?!" came from up in the turret. "What the fuck was that?"

No one was hurt, just a jolted driver and more NVGS being turned back on. Crisp chatter came over the radio. They confirmed with SFC Gilliard. Parked in an idling Humvee that had just taken a sub-carriage hit, it dawned on Perchigh— some motherfucker had just tried to kill them.

Leadership had seen it all; the truck, the explosion—the explosion rather that went down the moment Perchigh had wheeled parallel to a power- pole, the frantic egress of the detonator, who had, in his haste, outlandishly crashed.

By the time Perchigh had convinced himself that his team hadn't been wounded, the rear vehicle had backtracked, crossed a small bridge, and was pulling the Iraqi out by his eyebrows.

The whole platoon dismounted, setting up security or ogling at the damage the vehicle didn't take during their first, official IED strike. "Holy fuck!" Perchigh's squad leader came up saying. "You guys were engulfed! How the hell are you not hurt? ...you didn't see it? You were in this blooming onion of flames. It was up over the turret."

"They're bringin' his ass!" said a nearby platoon-mate, manning a radio. "The guy in that truck."

Perchigh hadn't heard any shots. *Good*, he thought, though he was unsure if his mirth was due to not having to take a life or his own cooling desire to go do it himself. SFC Gilliard had walked back over that bridge and was bringing the Iraqi up. The man was limping badly. His hands were zip-tied behind him.

On the order, the platoon spread out their vehicles. This included Perchigh's. As it turned out, the IED had been made almost entirely of C-3 and had owned no shrapnel to throw.

Perchigh marched up to the detainee. The man appeared maybe in his forties, shemagh on his head, off-white thobe covering an unimpressive body. He could have been the Iraqi Perchigh saw cleaning the toilets back on base. He was standing, wobbling, while SFC Gilliard held the zip-ties with one hand and blasted white-knuckled hooks into the Iraqi's head with the other.

Perchigh muzzle-thumped the detainee in the chest. Before he could follow up with a more concentrated volley, Gilliard hoisted the man upright then escorted him past a rabid platoon, tossing him into the platoon leader's Humvee with the interpreter waiting.

Soon after given to some pre-Abu Ghraib reception team, the detonator apparently provided a full confession. It was reported he had a multitude of injuries, to include a broken femur and blood coming out of his mouth and nose. 3rd Platoon's official report said it was from the crash.

That attack seemed to kick off a chain reaction. A symphony of IEDs became the norm, so frequent at one point they averaged three a day.

Eventually, one was not so harmless. This was the signature of the occupation era, indirect fire by way of roadside bombs. The crushing frustration was unbearable at times, and most would've given a month's pay to face those responsible. Some, two months.

But warfare is never fair, something Perchigh learned beyond any doubt. And the enemy fought it their way. There was nothing quite like doing a combat scavenger hunt, a hunt for the remains of a platoon-mate, once a weight-lifting monster, reduced to half a garbage bag by some chicken-shit dirty bomb that no one saw coming.

Despite the deadliness, despite the absurdity of trying to sell the world that America was spreading democracy, and despite the futility of handing out candy to kids whose parents were plotting their deaths, 3rd Platoon trudged and patrolled and wheeled in speeding Humvees. Onward until one had flipped into a canal, and Perchigh's ankle had paid for it.

...

An unpainted wall continued the cinder-block, mortar, cinder-block monotony. If there had been trees, surely they would have whizzed by this night, at least up until Gilliard got on the horn and initiated what was now their platoon's puttering crawl.

Perchigh was looking out his window. A string of Humvees full of weaponized men equaled a beauty to behold. The road that was leading 3rd Platoon to hopefully apprehend last night's Big Mouth had curved sharply, allowing Perchigh to see the three vehicles that still rolled on ahead.

Ever since the infamous "bongo truck incident," the platoon had begun a revolving roster, making sure which vehicle took point and which took rear always differed from one mission to the next. Improve the odds a little. Make 'em think. The whiz-wheel seemed fair, to say nothing of relieving. For all Perchigh's noticed stoicism—he'd grown secretly terrified of IEDs.

There hadn't been any on the way here, but the night was young, and if an enemy commo officer was so important, chances were likely protection would have been embedded.

"Roger," he said, including his call sign, then, "out."

He turned to the back, "One klick out."

"God damn, man," his RTO said.

The radio and its operator both sat directly behind Perchigh. He had punched the handset into the RTO's chest—anything to shut them up. For the past million cinder blocks, those two back there and even his knucklehead up in the turret kept on, in gleeful approval, about how Watts had randomly thermited some farmer's irrigation system.

The talk soon picked back up.

"He's from El Paso," the offended RTO said. "Went to some shit high school, too. Told me they kicked the ever-loving shit out of him, but how he was the only white kid who put up a fight. Over time, the bangers sort of respected him, how if a new Mexican showed up to school, acting all hard and shit, they'd sick Watts on 'em. He didn't always lose."

"Some vetting shit," said the turret.

"Oh, fuck yeah. Imagine. It's kinda like he was part of their gang."

"That's all bullshit." The SAW gunner said, "Watts used to live in Texas, but he didn't go to school there. He went to some private school. I can't remember where, but it wasn't Texas. Got expelled, though."

Composing himself and choosing to think of more immediate concerns, the medic had suggested that he stay off his ankle, but Perchigh would never stoop so low and swore the medic to secrecy. It helped that he was the only other Christian in the lot, a twice a year Presbyterian who couldn't recite a bible verse to save his life, but he was good at wrapping bandages and not reporting if one of the guys had a busted hoof.

Getting used to his wince, Perchigh, along with his team, soon stepped out and assumed their part in the growing cordon.

"Chest candy if we get that Big Mouth fucker, Perch," his SAW gunner looked over and said. Perchigh glanced. The team was all set. They were all looking at the patchwork of houses, separated from them by about thirty meters of dust.

There was something about the support role that can hurt worse than any busted ankle. You aren't practicing CQB. You aren't putting yourself in the fatal funnel…and you're jealous of the guys who are. All you could do, as Perchigh and his team did, was take a high-knee and listen to the radio and hopefully, the eruption of a little 7.62.

Now that's a fight! Improvised explosive devices, nobody would admit it in public, but to a man, 3rd Platoon would've rather checked out in a gunfight than be blown up by an old Russian mortar and a working cell phone.

House One was clear. So was House Two, and Three. Nothing. Soon reports came in, all delivering the same message: No weapons. No phones.

There were a number of detainees, though. Called to assist, Perchigh and his team held security on a row of groggy-eyed men. Women were allowed to remain inside, a tactic of the dapper platoon leader which drove some of the guys crazy.

One of the Iraqis had earned the leadership's attention quick. Perchigh always enjoyed when their platoon's ultimate leader showed his fangs. The other clean-cut bookworm in the group, when the lieutenant pinned a merchant or a farmer against a wall and slapped him silly, Perchigh felt an instant, undeniable comradery. A kindred spirit, forsaking officialdom for but a moment, laying into somebody who probably deserved more than what they'd get.

A few slaps later, the LT disappeared into House Two with his prisoner. Perchigh and his guys watched as the terp followed. The terp was from Baghdad, had taught something at some university, and now was getting paid to go off on whomever the LT or Gilliard sicked him on.

The night darkened. Stars didn't. One of Perchigh's men found a convenient rock to mindlessly kick around until a squad leader noticed and went in for a whispered speech on discipline.

Perchigh would have beaten his superior to the tongue-lashing if he hadn't been so absorbed in what had become an ongoing interrogation.

"Ask him again," the platoon leader demanded. There was concentrated confident Arabic. Then there were responding mumbles. Finally, it was out; passed down the chain until Perchigh gathered his team around their Humvee.

"Target's not here. Terp says he got wind of the Humvee-in-the-canal thing, believe it or not, and pulled up stakes." The team laughed. Perchigh did too. They showed every wartime emotion a team could—especially disappointment. Looking below the steadied rim of his SAW gunner's helmet, Perchigh assured them: "Don't worry, they said he relocated. LT is looking at it now. It's a village, and apparently only ten klicks from here."

The next day they all dismounted, the whole platoon. 1st Squad led a patrol under the full weight of the sun. Talk about diminishing goals, Higher wanted to mix this third go at Big Mouth with a little hearts and minds. It wasn't only daylight, it was broad daylight, that oppressive Iraq heat that reflected off the desert as to ignite cigarettes in packs or the stubble off face's who'd "forgotten" to shave.

Annoying was the topic, annoying as it was consistent: Perchigh's ankle had pulsed black and blue in the morning, and a wrap did what it could now to keep him walking. Some would call this a form of masochism, but some also would rather die than be labeled malingerer, coping out of patrol, especially when they had a team under them.

It always amazed Perchigh how orders could get so convoluted. If there were moments when he considered doing a full twenty, they were almost certainly shot down by moments like the one unfolding. A phantom ping, supposedly confirming the slapped-silly Iraqi hadn't been lying, supposedly had put Big Mouth in this village. Larger than the village the night before, kids had rushed out to greet them.

Kids: a good sign. Ambushes didn't happen when dirt-faced boys came up kicking soccer balls or when little hands surrounded to grip and grope government- issued candy.

Perchigh sighed and dug into his cargo pocket to begin passing out peanut M&Ms.

"Screw it," Watts said behind him. The pest had infiltrated Perchigh's team, yet to be yelled at by Gilliard because the twenty-year-man was too busy untangling the newest convolution over the radio.

How the heck does he do it? If anyone else pulled this kind of stunt, every squad leader would see it in two seconds. "Go back to your team, Watts."

Perchigh was ignored.

The platoon patrolled, down streets, doing what one does when not aiming to get lit up from a rooftop.

Kids were given coveted yellow bags. "Man, fuck these kids." Watts said.

Perchigh spun around. "Watts, I told you. I won't tell your ass again."

"Ass!" he brightened, sounding astounded, like a secret behind the word could rain down a prize and red balloons. "The preacher cusses. Well, holy fuckin' shit." Perchigh glanced at the throng of kids who'd gathered. They understood no English, but it irked him nonetheless. "Oh, wait-wait, you referring to, like, the biblical ass? Like what pre-bronze age goat herders rode around on when not spreading fairy tales?"

Perchigh was in his mouth, looking down on the little shit. "I think I'd blast *your* ass, right here, right now, if it wasn't for all the eyeballs."

Those who've been there know; wartime beefs can be big ones. Not everyone gets along, and there are reasons that don't make the VFW banner why some "brothers" don't talk for thirty or more years.

With a tone that flew as far beyond *Hooah* as his previous had fallen short of respect, but just as inspired, "That's the killer instinct we need, Perch," was all Watts said, fading behind a sand-blasted wall.

Word soon came down and spread that finding Big Mouth—a man who helped kill people—needed to take a backseat to some more diplomacy. A handful of grunts tasked with such emasculation was bound to be riddled with foul jokes, and an even fouler mood.

"Hey, Perch, check out the cross-eyed kid," his SAW gunner yelled.

"Take the candy, little goat fucker."

"Taste good?" Even Perchigh's own squad leader was unable to resist. "Yeah, good, 'cuz I killed your daddy." The crude meter had been turned, way up. An entire platoon was about to pop off because cogent orders liked to be derailed.

"Mistah," times enumerable was the reply, tearing into bags or running off to avoid larger children.

One such child must've been the cross-eyed one. The SAW gunner was a good soldier, but not one Perchigh would call terribly astute. It was always strange, or maybe *stranger*, seeing an albino kid in a place where the sweltering heat was like a furnace to crawl through. In these areas, they'd seen a few. Now it was time for another oddity, an Iraqi kid with a severe case of Down syndrome.

What life must've been like for him, this boy waddling up to Perchigh without a care in the world. Was it better or worse in a place like this, that, *what?* Perchigh thought, that he didn't know how crappy life truly was? How crappy *his* life was? Here was someone placed on earth to do little more than grow up a ragged weed in the cracks of a war zone.

Maudlin Sunday school teachers really ought to come here. Crude windows on worse walls mean- mugged, and sand kicked up like hornets. A few klicks through an Iraqi town was enough to shut up the most ardent cheeseball.

Were all men really endowed with love for their fellow creatures? It was as if the other children had been told by an adult not to walk near the poor kid.

From an exaggerated distance, others snickered at the boy; one picked up a rock then put it back down. Others wore faces caught between anticipation and a weird type of fear. *Poor kid.*

Yet the poor kid smiled. He kept smiling, gifted with a soul which a fallen world could only call disabled. The approaching boy was no more in a war than were the birds chirping on the wires above.

There could be no war in eyes that glittered spring, glittered the faithfulness of Perchigh's old hound back home, or those which come to us with complete, utter acceptance. Perchigh smiled and pulled out his last bag of M&Ms.

The boy's face exploded.

"Watts!" Perchigh cried, wiping the red heat that had sprayed him.

"Get the fuck back!" Watts said from over his sights.

"What the—what the fuck is wrong with you?!" Perchigh was on him, breaking those rotten teeth with every knuckle. Or at least he would have if his ankle hadn't tweaked during the charge and sent him sprawling. "You piece of shit," he cried.

He was going to pay for this. Watts. There was no joker's luck now. No globe to hide someone from sheer, reckless evil. The motherfucker ran up, now trying to drag Perchigh away by the high rear handle of his flak jacket.

"Let go—let goa me!"

Watts was saying something over and over. Perchigh took a high, wide swing. His knuckles connected with something hard. He swung again.

"Look at his chest, look at his chest." Before Perchigh could shift his rage from the sight of Watts' face to the flopping boy whose brains covered the street, an explosion laid them both flat. The biggest IED Perchigh ever saw, in all his time overseas, would come from a rigged retarded boy, covering him and Watts in clots of flying gore.

3rd Platoon soon swarmed the miserable village, haunting every face who'd stared, every window that had owned the faintest glimpse upon where a kid was sent unknowingly to a grim death.

Late in the afternoon, SFC Gilliard came to the Humvee that Perchigh had sat in, missing the tossing of beds and the righteous kill their most junior man got when some fuck had reached for an AK. The platoon sergeant held up a large Ziploc full of phones.

Whoever detonated that kid had done so remotely. No shock, not even when, on the highest authority, it came out later that it was believed the caller had been the very man who ended up eluding them yet again.

A phone and a boy.

A caller and a little torso that had been strapped with TNT.

And a few wires exposed, that one soldier had seen.

Joseph Perchigh's ankle got him the demotion he'd feared; idle misery behind the wire, but only for a couple of weeks. During which, CAG killed Big Mouth. The platoon got to serve in a cordon role, and the skies lit ablaze when a few Muj bodyguards finally thought it best to abandon their leader and scramble frantically into the sites of a well-armed, well pissed-off firing squad.

In six months, Joe Watts would receive his first demotion, knocking him not behind the wire but back to Private. First, though, he was to be awarded two medals, one for his role in the barrel-melting gunfire Perchigh wished he'd witnessed. The other for a single, well-aimed shot he wished he hadn't.

The Bar
USA 2015

The barroom still clanks with bottles, still stinks of sweat and stale pretzels littering a floor. Perchigh can't smell or hear, though. Not now. "You're not going to believe this," he says.

"What?" Ruiz goes for the letter.

"That's it," Preston says, beating him to it and snatching the paper so he can read it aloud: "Hope the rent-a-drunk I paid sent me off in style, Elle Oh Elle." Preston looks up at the others.

Ruiz is looking at him. "Okay…"

"Doc," Perchigh says, staring at him the way someone does right before saying something somber and slow. "Read the rest."

"Hey, Fuckos," Preston continues, imitating Watts. "Perch, Preston, and Mr. Chair Force Ruiz, the three amigos I knew would come. Guess what, I'm not dead. In heaven, maybe? Wanna join? Of course, you do. Caribbean island. Pussy. Tree. Where the beer flows like wine. We can get a bucket of holy water for Perch. Flights tonight-"

"What?!" Ruiz turns heads.

Perchigh opens the brown envelope, wider. He looks inside. He pulls out three tickets.

Doc laughs. He laughs, and he cries, and he looks back down at the letter. "Flights tonight. I had all your passports info already. Don't ask. Actually, do, just when we are drunk and on the beach." Doc's tone changes, falling into cadence with the words as their scribbler intended. "Hey, guys. Thanks for coming. Good times. Bad. Chutes and ladders. How it goes. Who knows what we can and can't prevent. But I know one thing. Life is frail and beautiful and fucked up and precious. Like those up-the-ass fortunately, unfortunately books we had to read in school." Doc looks up at Ruiz, then at Perch, "the little shit's alive."

"Alive and well!" Ruiz breathes. He goggles at the letter. "Anything else?"

Doc turns the paper so Ruiz can see. Floating below the last line is a cartoon dick and a smiling ghost, and a final moniker, barely on the page: UPZ N DOWNZ, BOYZ.

•••

Seats A1, 2, and 3. "He must be selling dope down there," Perchigh laughs, sliding into the aisle seat. Ruiz is riding bitch. An air force joke surfaces. Doc is looking out the window.

"Dude, this is insane," Ruiz says. "I don't know if I'm going to kiss or kill him."

A chocolate-skinned flight attendant appears and unleashes a hot accent on the three of them, "gentleman, seats upright before takeoff. Dank you."

"Can we order drinks?" Ruiz nudges Doc.

"Shit yeah," Doc says, revived. "This first-class shit's becoming a thing."

The three watch as people of profoundly less luck slog past to sit somewhere in the nether reaches back there in economy. Americans already dressed in Hawaiian shirts, giggling and spellbound, ready to start that vacation or celebrate that long-overdue divorce.

Two drinks come. The black angel has delivered; two glasses full to the rim with Coke and whiskey. Their plane speeds down the runway before the ice can melt.

Somewhere over the saltwater the plane begins to cough.

Masks drop down.

Flight attendants attend.

People scream.

The plane doesn't own the screens: the ones that let doomed passengers see how close they made it to a safe and dry and not-obliterated-on-the-surface- of-the-sea landing.

The three men sit. None put on their masks.

Just before the initial, nuts-rattling shake that made turbulence nothing and one attendant lose her shit, Doc and Ruiz had been handed their umpteenth round.

Now, Ruiz holds both.

Doc is back out the window. The moon shines on the ocean like a shimmering blanket.

People who won't make it to the resort dance-off run up and down the aisle. Mascara runs. Mouths run. Sand in so many hourglasses run, almost out, as the sea's shimmer draws near.

Ruiz holds up Doc's drink and looks at Perch. Eyes him for what feels like a long while. Perch grabs the drink and breathes in deeply, maybe even serene. "Screw it," he says.

~~Glossary~~

terms according to Watts

11B: The United States Army Military Occupational Specialty code for an enlisted Infantry soldier

18D: The United States Army Military Occupational Specialty code for a Special Forces medical sergeant

ANP: ~~Afghan National Police~~ watch your six—all I'm sayin

AO: Area of Operations

BP: ~~Blood pressure~~ like, no shit

C-3: Also known as Composition 3: a plastic explosive developed after World War II, and used during the Cold War. It can be molded into any shape, and run off a timer

CAG: Combat Applications Group, informally known as "Delta Force"

Class A: ~~Dress uniform for formal occasions~~ the most uncomfortable shit you'll ever wear

CO: ~~Commanding Officer~~ retread at the National War College and wife's a drunk

CONEX: ~~Container Express box~~ the large hot as shit fuckers we go in when an E-8 is looking for a 55 gallon drum of CLP

CQ: ~~In charge of quarters~~ sucks, usually 24 hours of sitting at a desk or patrolling the barracks

CQB: ~~Close Quarters Battle~~ we got to do more in the beginning, then came all the sexual harassment briefings and power points on drunk driving

DFAC: Dining facility

FOB: Forward Operating Base HALO: High Altitude, Low Opening

HESCO: A modern gabion primarily used for flood control and military fortifications

HHC: ~~Headquarters and Headquarters Company~~ I don't even have to say it

IED: Improvised Explosive Device

IFAK: Individual First Aid Kit

LT: ~~Lieutenant~~ a boot who can't work a compass and has a degree in probably Animal Husbandry

LZ: Landing Zone

M4: A lighter and shorter variant of the M16A2 assault rifle. The M4 is a 5.56×45mm NATO, air-cooled, gas-operated, direct impingement, magazine-fed carbine.

MP: ~~Military Police~~ blue falcons

MRAP: Mine-Resistant Ambush Protected vehicle

MRE: ~~Meals Ready-to-Eat~~ not so bad

MWR: ~~Morale, Welfare and Recreation~~ hahahahahahahahahaha!!! Yeah right

NCO: ~~Non-commissioned officer~~ fun while it lasts

NVG: Night Vision Goggles

OCONUS: ~~Outside Contiguous United States~~ where life is lived!

OCS: ~~Officer Candidate School~~ hugs at the finish line and participation trophies

PJ: Air Force Pararescue

PKM: A 7.62×54mmR general-purpose machine gun designed in the Soviet Union

PT: ~~Physical Training~~ what the guy in charge of you needs to do more of

QRF: ~~Quick Response/Reaction Force~~ usually the day off

RPG: ~~Rocket Propelled Grenade~~ Russian shit my boy tried to smuggle back but got popped

RTB: Return to base

RTO: Radio/Telephone Operator

SAW: ~~Squad Automatic Weapon~~ usually what the shitbag who can't shoot has to carry

SERE: Survival Evasion Resistance Escape

SFC: ~~Sergeant First Class~~ *either die a hero, or live long enough to become the villain*

SITREP: Situation Report

TIC: ~~Troops in contact~~ *what guys in the sky apparently call fire fights*

TOC: Tactical Operations Center

TQ: Al Taqaddum Airbase (Arabic: قدعا ق مدق ت لا الجولا), or Al Taqaddum (Called TQ in military shorthand slang), is an airbase that is located in central Iraq, approximately 74 kilometers west of Baghdad.

USAF: ~~United States Air Force~~ *said guys in sky* VFW: ~~Veterans of Foreign Wars~~ *those run down ass places hoisting signs for Bingo*

WIA: Wounded in Action *never know what's in store, do your best, cuz you control so little*